THE VELVETEEN RABB

Illustrated by Elena Kucharik
Adapted by Jennifer Boudart

Louis Weber, C.E.O.
Publications International, Ltd.
7373 North Cicero Avenue
Lincolnwood, Illinois 60646

Manufactured in U.S.A.

ISBN: 0-7853-1921-2

PUBLICATIONS INTERNATIONAL, LTD.
Stories to Grow On is a trademark of Publications International, Ltd.

Christmas morning! The boy could hardly sleep thinking about all of the wonderful presents he would receive. Normally the boy's stocking was filled with candy, but this year it held a wonderful surprise: a velveteen rabbit. The boy kissed the rabbit and squeezed its soft, squishy tummy. He held his new friend under his arm while he opened his other gifts. That Christmas the boy received many new toys which joined his old toys in the nursery. With so many new toys, the boy forgot the velveteen rabbit for a time. But the rabbit did not forget how nice it felt to be held in the boy's arms.

The nursery was filled with many different sorts of toys. There was a shiny toy soldier, a bright sailboat, and a car that buzzed and moved. The velveteen rabbit felt plain next to these toys. He was nothing but fluff and stitches. Only the horse was shabbier. Though the horse was old and frayed, he was wise. "Flashy toys don't last," he said. "They break easily, and they don't have anything lovable inside. They'll never be real."

"Real? Does that mean being new forever?"

"No," explained the horse. "You become real after someone loves you for a long time. By then you are old and tattered, but that's okay. When you are real, you are truly beautiful!"

That night the boy asked his nanny for his toy dog which he liked to hold while he slept. The nanny was not in the mood to look for the dog, so she handed him the velveteen rabbit. "He'll help you get to sleep just fine," she said.

The boy took the rabbit and held him tightly next to him. The velveteen rabbit fit the crook of his arm much better than the dog, and the boy fell asleep quickly. The rabbit was a bit squashed, but he didn't mind. He loved being held so closely while the boy slept. Of all the toys in the nursery, the velveteen rabbit felt he was the most special.

From that night on, the velveteen rabbit looked forward to bedtime when the boy would hug him. They spent days together, too. The boy took the velveteen rabbit on picnics, gave him rides in the wheelbarrow, and played with him in the garden.

The velveteen rabbit's heart was filled with joy. He was so happy on the inside that he didn't notice how shabby he was becoming on the outside. The boy loved the velveteen rabbit so much that he took him everywhere he went. The rabbit's fur was getting dirty from so many trips outdoors. And the space between the velveteen rabbit's ears was beginning to wear thin from all the nights of being petted while the boy drifted off to sleep.

One afternoon the boy left the velveteen rabbit hiding in the garden while he went to pick berries. Suddenly lightning flashed, and it began to rain. The frightened boy ran straight home. At bedtime he realized the velveteen rabbit was still outside. Who would rescue him? Nanny, of course!

Grumbling, she headed out with her flashlight and found the velveteen rabbit. With a scowl the nanny returned and said, "I can't believe I went out in the rain to find your silly toy!"

The boy snatched the rabbit from her. "He is not a toy! He's real!" he cried. The velveteen rabbit was cold and dripping with water, but he didn't mind at all. He was real!

One day the boy placed the velveteen rabbit on a comfortable bed of leaves while he went to play in the woods. Two strange creatures appeared. They looked like rabbits, but they had twitching noses and hopped by themselves. "Hello!" said one. "Would you like to come play with us?"

"N-no thank you," stuttered the velveteen rabbit. He did not want the strangers to know that he could not hop like they could.

"He's not real," said the small rabbit to his friend. "He's just a toy!" As they hopped away, the velveteen rabbit watched and longed to follow.

Soon the velveteen rabbit forgot about the two rabbits he met in the woods. He was too busy having fun with the boy. By now, the velveteen rabbit was more tattered than ever. He left trails of stuffing wherever he went, but he didn't even notice.

One day the boy became ill, and everything changed. While he was sick, the velveteen rabbit stayed close to him. The velveteen rabbit spent days imagining all the fun they would have when the boy got well. Each night he whispered his plans into the boy's ear. The velveteen rabbit was sure he could make the boy feel better.

With the help of the velveteen rabbit, the boy got better. For a while things were wonderful, and they spent all their time together. Then something terrible happened. The boy and his family went on vacation, but the velveteen rabbit was left behind!

When the boy left, the velveteen rabbit began to cry, and a beautiful flower grew where his tears had fallen! The flower held a magical figure who said, "Hello, dear rabbit, your love for the boy has earned you the right to become real!"

"Wasn't I real already?" asked the rabbit.

"Only to the boy. Now, I will make you real to everyone!" Suddenly the rabbit could hop on his own.

When the boy returned home from his long vacation, he headed to the woods to play one day. As he was walking, the boy saw a rabbit who came right up to him. The rabbit's glossy fur coat had a dark patch over the left eye. "That's incredible," thought the boy. "He looks just like my old friend, the velveteen rabbit."

The boy smiled as he thought of all the fun times he had shared with the velveteen rabbit. He did not know that his friend had returned, a real rabbit at last, and was standing right in front of him. Though he could move on his own now, the rabbit would never forget the boy's love which helped him become real.

One to Grow On

Love

In this story the velveteen rabbit learned all about love. First he learned how good it feels to love and to be loved. The loving friendship that the boy and the velveteen rabbit shared made him feel great. The velveteen rabbit also learned that love can change things. When the boy was feeling ill, the velveteen rabbit's love helped him get better.

The story of the velveteen rabbit reminds us how wonderful loved ones are. No matter what, you know they always want the best for you.